Julia A. M Furbish

The Flower of Liberty

Julia A. M Furbish

The Flower of Liberty

ISBN/EAN: 9783337105648

Printed in Europe, USA, Canada, Australia, Japan

Cover: Foto ©Andreas Hilbeck / pixelio.de

More available books at **www.hansebooks.com**

THE

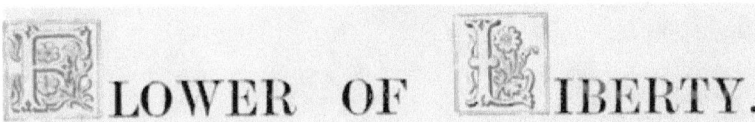

FLOWER OF LIBERTY.

Edited and Illustrated

By JULIA A. M. FURBISH.

BOSTON:

BENJAMIN B. RUSSELL, 55 CORNHILL.

PORTLAND, ME.: BAILEY AND NOYES.

CHICAGO, ILL.: S. S. BOYDEN.

1869.

CAMBRIDGE:

STEREOTYPED AND PRINTED BY JOHN WILSON AND SON.

Plates printed by the New England Lithographic Steam Printing Company, Boston.

INTRODUCTION.

HAVE thought that I could not make a more acceptable offering to gentlemen of the Army and Navy, and to all lovers of our glorious flag and the institutions which it symbolizes and protects, than the following collection from poets of world-wide renown, illustrated, though imperfectly, by my humble pencil.

During the first year of the war, when the mania for collecting Union designs for preservation was so prevalent in the loyal States, I thought that I would paint for *myself*, in water colors, a volume of national designs; knowing that I could thus, at my leisure and as fancy might dictate, make a more original and artistic collection than could be gathered from the numerous designs to be met with here and there, and which, having been published at slight expense, were of necessity wanting in beauty of coloring, and were, in most cases, imperfect in drawing.

I began the work in **1861,** painting the pictures as
they were suggested by the different emblems that ap-
peared during the war, and anxiously watching for every
new phase of loyalty that might furnish material for my
purpose. My work was a little more than a third finished
when the surrender of General Lee matured the half-
formed plan I had made three years previous; namely, to
complete it for publication as soon as peace should be
restored. I opened a correspondence with the authors
whose names will be found in the volume; and received
from them the most generous and flattering proofs of
their interest in the proposed work, in the form either
of original or revised poems, adapted to my drawings.
Suitably to requite them all for the favors bestowed
upon me, is not in my power; yet gratitude to them and
respect for myself require that I should at least offer
them the reasonable service of sincere and hearty thanks.
And here let me express my deep regret that several
valuable offerings for this work have either been received
too late, or have been excluded for want of time on my
part to prepare suitable illustrations. I am most grateful for the kindness of Senator Sumner, which enables
me to give a sketch of the cane once belonging to our
martyr-President, recently presented to him by Mrs.
Lincoln, and bearing the beautiful design of the eagle
shielding her nest of eaglets, with the folds of the flag,

from the approach of a serpent. Also would I acknowledge my indebtedness to others, whose designs in different forms have aided me so materially in the illustration
of this volume.

It has been suggested, that it would be well to have
in the collection *one* representation, at least, of our banner, "all tattered and torn;" but, on reflection, I shrank
from the thought of thus helping to commemorate the
fact that it had been insulted by those who had solemnly
sworn to keep it flying in the face of all foes without and
foes within. I chose rather to regard it as a thing of
divine life, which, though trampled on for a while, will,
from its inherent self-restoring power, rise again, and, in
company with him from whose teachings it sprang and
blossomed into the Flower of Liberty, will, to the end
of time and throughout the world, keep pace with the
progress of Christianity and equal rights. After four
years of as heroic bravery in deadly combat as was ever
recorded of the embattled hosts of Alexander, Cæsar,
Napoleon, or Wellington, it now shakes out its triumphant folds over all the late rebellious States of the
Union. It waves, alas! over rivers and seas, over moun-
tains and plains, crimsoned with the blood of many
thousands of gallant and noble young men, —

> "Whose souls, like setting suns,
> Have left their radiance flung on sea and shore."

But, although their earthly tabernacle has been destroyed, they still live: and thank God that, through their instrumentality, the integrity of their beloved country has been maintained; and that they, as glorified spirits, can now "behold the gorgeous ensign of the republic, known and honored throughout the earth, streaming in its original lustre, not a stripe erased or polluted, nor a single star obscured, bearing for its motto, spread all over in characters of living light, blazing on all its ample folds, as they float over the sea and over the land, and in every wind under the whole heavens, the sentiment, dear to every true American heart, — 'Liberty and Union, now and for ever, one and inseparable.'"

JULIA A. M. FURBISH.

PORTLAND, ME.

CONTENTS.

		PAGE.
THE FLOWER OF LIBERTY	Oliver Wendell Holmes	9
FORT WAGNER: 1863.—WHO SHALL VOTE? 1865.	George William Curtis	11
LAUS DEO!	John G. Whittier	12
"NOT YET"	William Cullen Bryant	15
ACCOMPLICES: VIRGINIA, 1865.	Thomas Bailey Aldrich	17
TO THE AMERICAN PEOPLE	Bayard Taylor	18
CHRISTMAS BELLS	Henry W. Longfellow	21
GOD OF PEACE	Rev. John Pierpont	23
KEEP STEP WITH THE MUSIC OF UNION	William Ross Wallace	24
OUR FLAG	T. W. Parsons	27
VOLUNTARIES	Ralph Waldo Emerson	29
THE SOLDIERS OF MEDUXNAKEAG	David Barker	30
STARS OF MY COUNTRY'S SKY	L. H. Sigourney	33
"LOVE ONE ANOTHER"	Harriet McEwen Kimball	35
THE HEART OF THE WAR	J. G. Holland	36
THE EAGLE OF CORINTH	Henry H. Brownell	41
OUR FLAG	Kate Putnam	47
EXODUS	Mrs. Adeline D. T. Whitney	49
THE COLOR-BEARER	J. T. Trowbridge	51
FLAG OF THE CONSTELLATION	T. Buchanan Read	55
PEACE	H. E. Prescott	57
THE FLAG	Julia Ward Howe	58
"OUR GUIDING STARS"	Orpheus C. Kerr	62
THE WAR-EAGLE	John Neal	64
"QUAKER LOYALTY"	John G. Whittier	66
THE HERO OF LAKE ERIE	Henry Theodore Tuckerman	67
THE FLAG	George H. Boker	72

CONTENTS.

			PAGE
THE SHIP OF STATE	. . . .	Henry W. Longfellow	. . . 74
NATIONAL ANTHEM: GOD OF THE FREE	. . .	William Ross Wallace	. . . 75
THE FLAG	. . . .	Lucy Larcom	 77
AFTER ALL	. . . .	William Winter	 79
THE UNION, — RIGHT OR WRONG	. . . . .	George P. Morris	 81
THE FLAG	. . . .	B. P. Shillaber	 83
OUR LAND AND ITS MEMORIES	. . . . . .	Charles T. Brooks	. . . 85
AMERICA	. . . .	Charles K. Tuckerman	. . . 89
WOUNDED UNTO DEATH	. . . .	Charles A. Barry	 92
THE OLD BLUE COAT	. . . .	Bishop Burgess	 95
THE EMPTY SLEEVE	. . . .	David Barker	 99
OUR FLAG	. . . .	Orpheus C. Kerr	. . . 101
UNION AND LIBERTY	. . . .	Oliver Wendell Holmes	. . . 106
OUR COUNTRY	. . . .	Harriet McEwen Kimball	. . . 108
THE OLD FLAG OVER-SEA	. . . .	Henry Morford	 110
PÆAN FOR VICTORY	. . . .	Edward P. Nowell	 115
THE FLAG	. . . .	J. Rollin M. Squire	 117
AFTER THE WAR	. . . .	Mrs. Ann S. Stephens	. . . 119
THE GREAT BELL ROLAND	. . . .	Theodore Tilton	 121
SPIRIT OF THE UNION SOLDIERS	. . . . . .	Miles O'Reilly	 125
PEACE	. . . .	Phœbe Cary	 127
UNION	. . . .	Albert Laighton	 129
ABRAHAM LINCOLN	. . . .	Mrs. Julia Ward Howe	. . . 130

The Flower of Liberty.

BY OLIVER WENDELL HOLMES.

WHAT flower is this that greets the morn,
Its hues from heaven so freshly born?
With burning star and flaming band
It kindles all the sunset-land, —
O, tell us what its name may be!
Is this the Flower of Liberty?
It is the banner of the free,
The starry Flower of Liberty!

In savage Nature's far abode
Its tender seed our fathers sowed:
The storm-winds rocked its swelling bud,
Its opening leaves were streaked with blood,
Till, lo, earth's tyrants shook to see
The full-blown Flower of Liberty!
Then hail the banner of the free,
The starry Flower of Liberty!

[9]

Behold! its streaming rays unite —
One mingling flood of braided light —
The red that fires the Southern rose
With spotless white from Northern snows,
And, spangled o'er its azure sea,
The sister stars of Liberty!
Then hail the banner of the free,
The starry Flower of Liberty!

The blades of heroes fence it round;
Where'er it springs is holy ground:
From tower and dome its glories spread;
It waves where lonely sentries tread;
It makes the land as ocean free,
And plants an empire on the sea:
Then hail the banner of the free,
The starry Flower of Liberty!

Thy sacred leaves, fair Freedom's flower,
Shall ever float on dome and tower,
To all their heavenly colors true,
In blackening frost or crimson dew, —
And God love us as we love thee,
Thrice holy Flower of Liberty!
Then hail the banner of the free,
The starry Flower of Liberty!

Fort Wagner: 1863. — Who shall Vote? 1865.

BY GEORGE WILLIAM CURTIS.

 LIVING cloud of mingled hue
　　Across the sand impetuous came,
　Into a fiery whirlwind grew,
　　And dashed against the fort in flame.

One purpose in each steady heart;
　One light in every solemn eye:
"Brothers, alive we do not part;
　We die together, if we die."

They fought together, black and white;
　They fell together, true and brave;
They died together in the fight;
　They rest together in one grave.

One blood, one faith, one hope, they shared;
　One right with us their brethren share:
To die for us those heroes dared;
　To wrong their brothers do we dare?

Laus Deo!

BY JOHN G. WHITTIER.

On hearing the bells ring for the Constitutional Amendment abolishing Slavery in the
United States.

T is done!
  Clang of bell and roar of gun
  Send the tidings up and down.
How the belfries rock and reel!
How the great guns, peal on peal,
Fling the joy from town to town!

  Ring, O bells!
Every stroke exulting tells
Of the burial-hour of crime.
  Loud and long, that all may hear,
  Ring for every listening ear
Of Eternity and Time!

  Let us kneel!
God's own voice is in that peal,
And this spot is holy ground.
  Lord, forgive us! What are we,
  That our eyes this glory see,
That our ears have heard the sound!

For the Lord
On the whirlwind is abroad;
In the earthquake he has spoken:
He has smitten with his thunder
The iron walls asunder,
And the gates of brass are broken!

Loud and long
Lift the old exulting song;
Sing with Miriam by the sea:
He hath cast the mighty down;
Horse and rider sink and drown;
He hath triumphed gloriously!

Did we dare,
In our agony of prayer,
Ask for more than he has done?
When was ever his right hand,
Over any time or land,
Stretched as now beneath the sun?

How they pale,
Ancient myth and song and tale,
In this wonder of our days,
When the cruel rod of war
Blossoms white with righteous law,
And the wrath of man is praise!

Blotted out!
All within, and all about,
Shall a fresher life begin;
Freer breathe the universe
As it rolls its heavy curse
On the dead and buried sin !

It is done!
In the circuit of the sun
Shall the sound thereof go forth.
It shall bid the sad rejoice,
It shall give the dumb a voice,
It shall belt with joy the earth!

Ring and swing
Bells of joy! on morning's wing
Send the song of praise abroad;
With a sound of broken chains,
Tell the nations that He reigns
Who alone is Lord and God !

"Not Yet."

BY WILLIAM CULLEN BRYANT.

COUNTRY, marvel of the earth !
    O realm to sudden greatness grown !
The age that gloried in thy birth,
    Shall it behold thee overthrown ?
Shall traitors lay that greatness low ?
No: land of hope and blessing, no !

And we, who wear thy glorious name,
    Shall we, like cravens, stand apart,
When those whom thou hast trusted aim
    The death-blow at thy generous heart ?
Forth goes the battle-cry, and lo !
Hosts rise in harness, shouting no !

And they who founded in our land
    The power that rules from sea to sea,
Bled they in vain, or vainly planned
    To leave their country great and free ?
Their sleeping ashes, from below,
Send up the thrilling murmur, no !

Knit they the gentle ties which long
 These sister States were proud to wear,
And forged the kindly links so strong,
 For idle hands in sport to tear, —
For scornful hands aside to throw?
No: by our fathers' memory, no!

Our humming marts, our iron ways,
 Our wind-tossed woods on mountain crest;
The hoarse Atlantic, with his lays,
 The calm broad ocean of the West,
And Mississippi's torrent flow,
And loud Niagara, answer, no!

Not yet the hour is nigh, when they
 Who deep in Eld's dim twilight sit,
Earth's ancient kings, shall rise and say,
 "Proud country, welcome to the pit:
So soon art thou, like us, brought low?"
No: sullen groups of shadows, no!

For now, behold the arm that gave
 The victory in our fathers' day,
Strong as of old to guard and save, —
 That mighty arm which none can stay,
On clouds above and fields below,
Writes in men's sight, the answer, no!

Accomplices: Virginia, 1863.

BY THOMAS BAILEY ALDRICH.

THE soft new grass is creeping o'er the graves
      By the Potomac; and the crisp ground-flower
      Lifts its blue cup to catch the passing shower;
The pine-cone ripens, and the long moss waves
Its tangled gonfalons above our braves.

   Hark, what a burst of music from yon bower! —
   The Southern nightingale that, hour by hour,
In its melodious summer madness raves.
Ah! with what delicate touches of her hand,
   With what sweet voices, Nature seeks to screen
The awful Crime of this distracted land, —
   Sets her birds singing, while she spreads her green
Mantle of velvet where the Murdered lie,
As if to hide the horror from God's eye!

2

To the American People.

BY BAYARD TAYLOR.

HAT late, in half-despair, I said,
   " The Nation's ancient life is dead;
      Her arm is weak, her blood is cold;
She hugs the peace that gives her gold, —
The shameful peace, that sees expire
Each beacon-light of patriot-fire,
And makes her court a traitor's den:"
Forgive me this, my countrymen!

Oh! in your long forbearance grand,
Slow to suspect the treason planned,
Enduring wrong, yet hoping good,
For sake of olden brotherhood;
How grander, how sublimer far
At the roused eagle's call ye are,
Leaping from slumber to the fight
For Freedom and for Chartered Right!

NORTH — WIDE AWAKE.

Throughout the land there goes a cry;
A sudden splendor fills the sky;
From every hill the banners burst,
Like buds by April breezes nurst:
In every hamlet, home, and mart,
The fire-beat of a single heart
Keeps time to strains whose pulses mix
Our blood with that of Seventy-Six!

The shot whereby the old flag fell
From Sumter's battered citadel
Struck down the lines of party creed,
And made ye one in soul and deed, —
One mighty People, stern and strong,
To crush the consummated wrong;
Indignant with the wrath whose rod
Smites as the awful sword of God!

The cup is full!   They thought ye blind;
The props of state they undermined;
Abused your trust, your strength defied,
And stained the Nation's name of pride.
Now lift to heaven your loyal brows,
Swear once again your fathers' vows,
And cut through traitor hearts a track
To nobler fame and freedom back!

Draw forth your million blades as one;
Complete the battle then begun!
God fights ·with ye, and overhead
Floats the dear banner of your dead:
They, and the glories of the Past,
The Future dawning dim and vast,
And all the holiest hopes of man,
Are beaming triumph in your van!

Slow to resolve, be swift to do!
Teach ye the False how fight the True!
How bucklered Perfidy shall feel
In her black heart the Patriot's steel;
How sure the bolt that Justice wings;
How weak the arm a traitor brings;
How mighty they who steadfast stand
For Freedom's Flag and Freedom's Land!

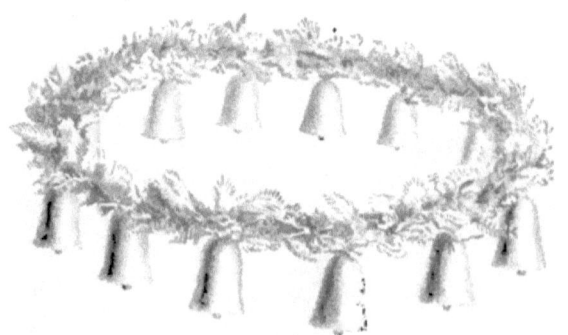

Christmas Bells.

BY HENRY W. LONGFELLOW.

HEARD the bells on Christmas Day
Their old familiar carols play,
        And wild and sweet
        The words repeat
Of peace on earth, good-will to men!

I thought how, as the day had come,
The belfries of all Christendom
        Had rolled along
        The unbroken song
Of peace on earth, good-will to men

Till, ringing, singing on its way,
The world revolved from night to day
        A voice, a chime,
        A chant sublime
Of peace on earth, good-will to men!

Then from each black, accursèd mouth,
The cannon thundered in the South,
        And with the sound
        The carols drowned
Of peace on earth, good-will to men!

It was as if an earthquake rent
The hearthstones of a continent,
    And made forlorn
    The households born
Of peace on earth, good-will to men!

And in despair I bowed my head:
"There is no peace on earth," I said;
    "For hate is strong,
    And mocks the song
Of peace on earth, good-will to men!"

Then pealed the bells more loud and deep:
"God is not dead; nor doth he sleep!
    The Wrong shall fail,
    The Right prevail,
With peace on earth, good-will to men!"

God of Peace.

BY THE REV. JOHN PIERPONT.

GOD of Peace! whose spirit fills
All the echoes of our hills,
All the murmurs of our rills,
　　Now the storm is o'er: —
Oh, let freemen be our sons;
And let future Washingtons
Rise to lead their valiant ones,
　　Till there's war no more!

By the patriot's hallowed rest,
By the warrior's gory breast,
Never let our graves be pressed
　　By a despot's throne:
By the Pilgrim's toils and cares,
By their battles and their prayers,
By their ashes, let our heirs
　　Bow to thee alone.

Keep Step with the Music of Union.

BY WILLIAM ROSS WALLACE.

KEEP step with the music of Union!
   The music our ancestors sung
   When States, like a jubilant chorus,
   To beautiful sisterhood sprung.
Oh! thus shall their great Constitution,
  That guards all the homes of the land,
A mountain of freedom and justice
  For millions eternally stand.
North and South, East and West, all unfurling
  ONE banner alone o'er the sod;
ONE voice from America swelling
  In worship of Liberty's God.

Keep step with the music of Union!
  'Tis thus we shall nourish the light
Our fathers lit for the chained nations
  That darkle in Tyranny's night.

The blood of the whole world is with us,
  O'er ocean by oligarchs hurled,
And they who would dare to attack us
  Shall sink with the wrath of a world.
     North and South, &c.

" Keep step with the music of Union ! "
  Our soldiers and sailor-boys shout,
While from their invincible cannon
  The thunders roll choruses out, —
" Down, down with all traitors polluting
  The world Freedom's God gave the Free !
The Flag of GRANT, FARRAGUT, ever
  Shall rule on the shore and the sea.
     North and South, &c."

" Keep step with the music of Union ! "
  Still LINCOLN, the glorified, cries;
The flames of the patriot flashing,
  Like lightning of heaven, from his eyes;
Red wrath on all copperhead demons
  Who dare trail their blasphemous slime
On Loyalty's thrice-sacred flowers,
  That WASHINGTON sowed in our clime!
     North and South, &c.

Keep step with the music of Union !
  All traitors shall sink at the sound;
But patriots march on to Heaven,
  With hallowèd harmony crowned:
Then cheer for the Past with its glory,
  For the resolute Present hurrah,
And shout for the starry-browed Future,
  With Virtue and Freedom and Law !
North and South, East and West, all unfurling
  ONE *banner alone o'er the sod;*
ONE *voice from America swelling*
  In worship of Liberty's God !

Our Flag.

BY T. W. PARSONS.

"Libertà va cercando, che è si cara!"
　　　　　　　　　　DANTE.
It waves for Liberty, that is so dear!

STILL proudest symbol on the seas,
　　Young banner of my native land!
The time is near when every breeze
　　By which thy starry folds are fanned

Shall bring the name of Freedom clear,
　　More clear than ever heard before,
To each expecting bondman's ear,
　　On every tyrant-trodden shore.

Beyond the fires of Hecla, thou
　　Shalt burn with no uncertain gleam,
And crowds of worshippers shall bow
　　To thee by many an orient stream.

Dull Egypt, startled in her fen,
    Shall hail thee fluttering in the Nile!
And fearless tribes of painted men
    Salute thee from their savage isle.

Wherever other flags may dare
    To carry new distress and wrong,
Thy radiant heraldry shall bear
    A token earth has looked for long.

The hues of heaven's prophetic bow
    Less beauteous then shall seem than thine;
Nor more of peace and hope bestow
    Than thy serene, fulfilling sign.

Voluntaries.

BY RALPH WALDO EMERSON.

FREEDOM, all winged, expands,
  Nor perches in a narrow place;
  Her broad van seeks unplanted lands;
  She loves a poor and virtuous race.
Clinging to a colder zone,
Whose dark sky sheds the snowflake down,
The snowflake is her banner's star,
Her stripes the boreal streamers are.
Freedom loves the Northman well.

The Soldiers of Meduxnakeag.

BY DAVID BARKER.

COME on with me now: let us travel on,
    Not far, — not many a league, —
From the spot where the old and the bold St. John
    Locks hands with Meduxnakeag.

As a pay or a fee for this stroll with me,
    I will tell you a tale to-day,
Of the wife, the widow, the mother, — all three, —
    And the soldiers, Robert Gray.

It was here, very near where we stroll to-day,
    Where the grim old barrack * stands,
That a girl in the pride of her youth, they say,
    With a Sergeant Gray locked hands.

But Death stole into those barrack walls,
    Which stood near the river's banks,
And entered the name of that Sergeant Gray
    On the list of his spectre ranks.

* At Houlton, Maine.

But the years rolled by at Meduxnakeag,
    When quick came a country's call
For the name of her own, of her manly boy,
    Through a rent in that barrack wall.

She bade him go forth from Meduxnakeag,
    To his God and his country true;
She bade him go forth, this young *Captain* Gray,
    Clad out in his Union blue.

He went: but he wandered not back again
    To the roof near the river's banks;
He went, like his father, old Sergeant Gray,
    To fill up Death's spectre ranks.

From the charge on that field,* that was steeping in
      gore,
    He went where the brave spirits dwell,
With "*No matter for me!*" and "Push on, my brave
      boys!"
    Ringing out o'er the shot and the shell.

What is that, crouching there in the barrack's nook,
    Bowed down by the hand of dismay?
There's a trace in her face of the laughing girl,—
    'Tis the mother of Robert Gray.

           * Fort Gilman, Sept. 28, 1864.

Let us leave the weird walls at Meduxnakeag:
  I'm too old and ashamed to cry,
And I feel that the tears are rushing fast
  For the crowsfeet round my eye.

But, my friends, if you worship a God in this life,
  And you ever kneel down to pray,
Remember the mother, the widow, the wife,
  Of the soldiers, Robert Gray.

Stars of my Country's Sky.

BY L. H. SIGOURNEY.

ARE ye all there? are ye all there,
　　Stars of my country's sky?
Are ye *all* there? *are ye all there,*
　　In your shining homes on high?
"Count us! count us!" was their answer,
　　As they darted on my view,
In glorious perihelion,
　　Amid their field of blue.

I cannot count ye rightly;
　　There's a cloud with sable rim:
I cannot make your number out,
　　For my eyes with tears are dim.
O bright and blessed angel!
　　On white wing floating by,
Help me to count, and not to miss
　　One star in my country's sky.

3

Then the angel touched mine eyelids,
　　And touched the frowning cloud;
And its sable rim departed,
　　And it fled with murky shroud.
There was no missing Pleiad
　　'Mid all that sister race:
The Southern Cross gleamed radiant forth,
　　And the Pole-star kept its place.

Then I knew it was the angel　.
　　Who woke the hymning strain
That, at our dear Redeemer's birth,
　　Pealed out o'er Bethlehem's plain;
And still its heavenly key-tone
　　My listening country held,
For all her constellated stars
　　The diapason swelled.

LOVE ONE ANOTHER.

"Love One Another."

BY HARRIET M°EWEN KIMBALL.

RE-UNITED, scourged yet blest,
　　Oh, let contention cease!
One your banner, one your crest,
　　Brothers, be at peace!

Sheathe the sword, rebellious South!
　　O North, bind up the wound!
Dead the thing that cursed ye both;
　　Let good-will abound!

Freedom, queen by right divine,
　　Her reign indeed begun!
Six and thirty stars shall shine
　　In her crown as one!

The Heart of the War.

BY J. G. HOLLAND.

PEACE in the clover-scented air,
  And stars within the dome;
And underneath, in dim repose,
  A plain New-England home.
Within, a murmur of low tones,
  And sighs from hearts oppressed,
Merging in prayer at last, that brings
  The balm of silent rest.

I've closed a hard day's work, Marty;
  The evening chores are done;
And you are weary with the house
  And with the little one.
But he is sleeping sweetly now,
  With all our pretty brood:
So come, and sit upon my knee,
  And it will do me good.

O Marty! I must tell you all
    The trouble in my heart;
And you must do the best you can
    To take and bear your part.
You've seen the shadow on my face,
    You've felt it day and night;
For it has filled our little home,
    And banished all its light.

I did not mean it should be so;
    And yet I might have known
That hearts that live as close as ours
    Can never keep their own.
But we are fallen on evil times;
    And, do whate'er I may,
My heart grows sad about the war,
    And sadder every day.

I think about it when I work,
    And when I try to rest;
And never more than when your head
    Is pillowed on my breast.
For then I see the camp-fires blaze,
    And sleeping men around,
Who turn their faces toward their homes,
    And dream upon the ground.

I think about the dear brave boys,
  My mates in other years,
Who pine for home and those they love,
  Till I am choked with tears.
With shouts and cheers they marched away
  On glory's shining track;
But ah, how long, how long they stay!
  How few of them come back!

One sleeps beside the Tennessee,
  And one beside the James;
And one fought on a gallant ship,
  And perished in its flames.
And some, struck down by fell disease,
  Are breathing out their life;
And others, maimed by cruel wounds,
  Have left the deadly strife.

Ah, Marty, Marty! only think
  Of all the boys have done
And suffered in this weary war, —
  Brave heroes every one.
Oh! often, often in the night,
  I hear their voices call, —
Come on, and help us!   Is it right
  That we should bear it all?

And when I kneel, and try to pray,
    My thoughts are never free,
But cling to those who toil and fight
    And die for you and me;
And, when I pray for victory,
    It seems almost a sin
To fold my hands, and ask for what
    I will not help to win.

Oh! do not cling to me and cry;
    For it will break my heart:
I'm sure you'd rather have me die
    Than not to bear my part.
You think that some should stay at home
    To care for those away;
But still I'm helpless to decide
    If I should go or stay.

For, Marty, all the soldiers love,
    And all are loved again;
And I am loved, and love perhaps
    No more than other men.
I cannot tell — I do not know —
    Which way my duty lies,
Or where the Lord would have me build
    My fire of sacrifice.

I feel — I know — I am not mean;
  And, though I seem to boast,
I'm sure that I would give my life
  To those who need it most.
Perhaps the Spirit will reveal
  That which is fair and right:
So, Marty, let us humbly kneel
  And pray to Heaven for light.

Peace in the clover-scented air,
  And stars within the dome;
And underneath, in dim repose,
  A plain New-England home.
Within, a widow in her weeds,
  From whom all joy is flown,
Who kneels among her sleeping babes,
  And weeps and prays alone.

The Eagle of Corinth.*

BY HENRY H. BROWNELL.

DID you hear of the fight at Corinth,
　　How we whipped out Price and Van Dorn?
　　(Ah! that day we earned our rations:
Our cause was God's and the Nation's,
　　Or we'd have come out forlorn!)
A long and a terrible day!
And at last, when night grew gray,
By the hundred there they lay
(Heavy sleepers, you'd say),
　　That wouldn't wake on the morn.

---

* "The finest thing I ever saw was a live American eagle, carried by the 8th Wisconsin Regiment, in the place of a flag. It would fly off over the enemy during the hottest of the fight; then would return, and seat himself upon his pole, clap his pinions, shake his head, and start again. Many and hearty were the cheers that arose from our lines as the old fellow would sail around, first to the right, then to the left, and always return to his post, regardless of the storm of leaden hail that was around him. Something seemed to tell us that that battle was to result in our favor; and, when the order was given to charge, every man went at them with fixed bayonets; and the enemy scattered in all directions, leaving us in possession of the battle-field." — *Letter from an Illinois Volunteer.*

6

Our staff was bare of a flag:
We didn't carry a rag
  In those brave marching days;
Ah, no! but a finer thing,
With never a cord or string, —
An Eagle, of ruffled wing,
  And an eye of awful gaze!

The grape — it rattled like hail;
  The minies were dropping like rain,
The first of a thunder-shower;
    The wads were blowing like chaff,
(There was pounding, like floor and flail,
  All the front of our line!)
So we stood it, hour after hour;
  But our eagle — he felt fine!
    'Twould have made you cheer and laugh,
To see, through that iron gale,
How the old Fellow'd swoop and sail
Above the racket and roar:
To right and to left he'd soar;
But ever came back, without fail,
  And perched on his standard staff.

All that day, I tell you true,
  They had pressed us, steady and fair,

Till we fought in street and square
(The affair, you might think, looked blue);
  But we knew we had them there!
Our works and batteries were few, —
Every gun, they'd have sworn, they knew;
But, you see, there was one or two
  We had fixed for them, unaware.

They reckon they've got us now!
  For the next half hour 'twill be warm.
Aye, aye; look yonder! — I vow,
If they weren't Secesh, how I'd love them!
  Only see how grandly they form
(Our eagle whirling above them)
  To take Robinett by storm!
  They're timing! — it can't be long —
Now for the nub of the fight!
  (You may guess that we held our breath.)
By the Lord! 'tis a splendid sight, —
  A column two thousand strong
  Marching square to the death!

On they came in solid column;
  For once, no whooping nor yell
(Ah! I dare say they felt solemn).
  Front and flank, grape and shell,

Our batteries pounded away!
And the minies hummed to remind 'em
   They had started on no child's play!
Steady they kept a-going,
But a grim wake settled behind 'em:
From the edge of the *abattis*
   (Where our dead and dying lay
Under fence and fallen tree)
   Up to Robinett, all the way
The dreadful swath kept growing!
   'Twas butternut flecked with gray.

Now for it, at Robinett!
Muzzle to muzzle we met
   (Not a breath of bluster or brag,
  Not a lisp for quarter or favor),
Three times, there by Robinett!
With a rush, their feet they set
On the logs of our parapet,
   And waved their bit of a flag:
  What could be finer or braver?
But our cross-fire stunned them in flank;
They melted, rank after rank;
(Over them, with terrible poise,
Our Bird did circle and wheel!)
   Their whole line began to waver, —

Now for the bayonet, boys!
  On them with the cold steel!

Ah, well! — you know how it ended:
  We did for them, there and then;
But their pluck throughout was splendid.
  (As I said before, I could love them!)
  They stood, to the last, like men:
Only a handful of them
  Found their way back again.
Red as blood, o'er the town,
The angry sun went down,
  Firing flagstaff and vane.
And our eagle, — as for him,
There, all ruffled and grim,
  He sat, o'erlooking the slain!

Next morning you'd have wondered
  How we had to drive the spade!
There, in great trenches and holes,
  (Ah, God rest their poor souls!)
We piled some fifteen hundred
  Where that last charge was made!

Sad enough, I must say!
  No mother to mourn and search,

No priest to bless or to pray:
We buried them where they lay,
   Without a rite of the church;
But our eagle, all that day,
   Stood solemn and still on his perch.
'Tis many a stormy day
Since, out of the cold, bleak North,
Our great War-Eagle sailed forth
To swoop o'er battle and fray.
Many and many a day
O'er charge and storm hath he wheeled,
Foray and foughten field,
    Tramp and volley and rattle!
Over crimson trench and turf,
Over climbing clouds of surf,
Through tempest and cannon-rack,
Have his terrible pinions whirled.
    (A thousand fields of battle!
  A million leagues of foam!)
But our bird shall yet come back:
   He shall soar to his Eyrie-Home,
And his thunderous Wings be furled,
In the gaze of a gladdened world,
   On the Nation's loftiest Dome

Our Flag.

BY KATE PUTNAM.

PEAL out, O bells! from jubilant throats,
　A sudden song of mirth!
Lo, where across our land it floats,
　The flower of all the earth!
More firmly are its roots inwrought
　With Love and Life, to-day,
Than when the grasp of Treason sought
　To rend its bloom away.

The blood of gallant hearts and true
　Has lent its crimson dye;
Its azure is the splendid blue
　Of Hope's unclouded sky;
And, blotting out the bitter Past,
　A People's tears of pain
Have washed its whiteness pure, at last,
　From Slavery's ancient stain.

Look down from your eternal height,
  Ye spirits tried and brave,
And crown with Heaven's refulgent light
  The flag ye died to save!
Look up, O living, loyal eyes!
  Where, every steady star
Undimmed within its native skies,
  Your standard shines afar!

Let reverent silence be its meed;
  Firm heart and prayerful breath:
What pæan can that glory need
  Whose power is proved by Death?
The grave that holds our Martyr-chief,
  The fields that hide our slain,
Shall voice a Nation's love and grief,
  Her triumph and her pain.

Oh, symbol-hope of all the world!
  The pledge of Liberty!
A stronger hand than ours unfurled
  Thy mighty prophecy.
Let all thy starry splendors shine!
  Chime, bells, in sweet accord!
Earth cannot harm that holy sign, —
  The banner of the Lord!

Exodus.

BY MRS. ADELINE D. T. WHITNEY.

HEAR ye not how, from all high points of Time, —
    From peak to peak, a-down the mighty chain
That links the ages, echoing sublime
        A voice almighty, — leaps one grand refrain,
Wakening the generation with a shout
And trumpet-call of thunder, — Come ye out!

Out from old forms and dead idolatries,
    From fading myths and superstitious dreams,
From Pharisaic rituals and lies,
    And all the bondage of the life that seems, —
Out, on the pilgrim-path of heroes trod
On earth's wastes, to reach forth after God!

The Lord hath bowed his heaven, and come down!
    Now, in this latter century of time,
Once more his tent is pitched on Sinai's crown;
    Once more in clouds must Faith to meet him climb;

4

Once more his thunder crashes on our doubt
And fear and sin, — My people, come ye out!

From false ambitions and base luxuries,
    From puny aims and indolent self-ends,
From cant of faith and shams of liberties,
    And mist of ill that Truth's day-beam lends, —
Out from all darkness of the Egypt-land,
Into thy sun-blaze on the desert sand!

" Leave ye your flesh-pots; turn from filthy greed
    Of gain, that doth the thirsting spirit mock, —
And heaven shall drop sweet manna for your need,
    And rain clear rivers from the unhewn rock."
Thus saith the Lord! and Moses, meek, unshod,
Within the cloud stands hearkening to his God.

Show us our Aaron, with his rod in flower;
    Our Miriam, with her timbrel-soul in tune!
And call some Joshua in the Spirit's power
    To poise our sun of strength at point of noon!
God of our fathers! on land and sea
Still keep our struggling footsteps close to Thee.

The Color-Bearer.

BY J. T. TROWBRIDGE.

'TWAS a fortress to be stormed:
    Boldly right in view they formed,
        All as quiet as a regiment parading:
Then in front a line of flame!
Then at left and right the same!
Two platoons received a furious enfilading.
    To their places still they filed,
    And they smiled at the wild
        Cannonading.

    " 'Twill be over in an hour!
    'Twill not be much of a shower!
Never mind, my boys," said he, "a little drizzling!"
    Then to cross that fatal plain,
    Through the whirring, hurtling rain
Of the grape-shot, and the minie-bullets' whistling!
    But he nothing heeds nor shuns,
    As he runs, with the guns
        Brightly bristling!

Leaving trails of dead and dying
In their track, yet forward flying
Like a breaker where the gale of conflict rolled them,
With a foam of flashing light
Borne before them on their bright
Burnished barrels, — oh, 'twas fearful to behold them!
While from ramparts roaring loud
Swept a cloud like a shroud
    To enfold them!

Oh, his color was the first!
Through the burying cloud he burst,
With the standard to the battle forward slanted!
Through the belching, blinding breath
Of the flaming jaws of Death,
Till his banner on the bastion he had planted!
By the screaming shot that fell,
And the yell of the shell,
    Nothing daunted.

Right against the bulwark dashing,
Over tangled branches crashing,
'Mid the plunging volleys thundering ever louder!
There he clambers, there he stands,
With the ensign in his hands, —

Oh! was ever hero handsomer or prouder?
   Streaked with battle-sweat and slime,
   And sublime in the grime
     Of the powder!

   'Twas six minutes, at the least,
   Ere the closing combat ceased, —
Near as we the mighty moments then could measure;
   And we held our souls with awe,
   Till his haughty flag we saw
On the lifting vapors drifting o'er the embrasure, —
   Saw it glimmer, in our tears,
   While our ears heard the cheers
     Rend the azure!

   Through the *abattis* they broke,
   Through the surging cannon-smoke,
And they drove the foe before like frightened cattle!
   Oh! but never wound was his;
   For in other wars than this,
Where the volleys of Life's conflict roar and rattle,
   He must still, as he was wont,
   In the front bear the brunt
     Of the battle.

   He shall guide the van of Truth!
   And in manhood, as in youth,

Be her fearless, be her peerless, Color-bearer!
   With his high and bright example,
   Like a banner brave and ample,
Ever leading, through receding clouds of Error,
   To the empire of the Strong;
   And to Wrong he shall long
      Be a terror!

Flag of the Constellation.

BY T. BUCHANAN READ.

THE stars of morn on our banner borne
    With the iris of heaven are blended;
    The hand of our sires first mingled those fires,
    And by us they shall be defended.
Then hail the true Red, White, and Blue, —
    The flag of the Constellation!
It sails, as it sailed by our forefathers hailed,
    O'er battles that made us a nation.

What hand so bold as strike from its fold
    One star or one stripe of its brightening!
For him be those stars each a fiery Mars,
    Each stripe be a terrible lightning:
Then hail the true Red, White, and Blue, —
    The flag of the Constellation!
It sails, as it sailed by our forefathers hailed,
    O'er battles that made us a nation.

Its meteor form shall ride the storm
  Till the fiercest of foes surrender;
The storm gone by, it shall gild the sky,
  A rainbow of peace and of splendor:
Then hail the true Red, White, and Blue, —
  The flag of the Constellation!
It sails, as it sailed by our forefathers hailed,
  O'er battles that made us a nation.

Peace to the world is our motto unfurled,
  Though we shun not the field that is gory:
At home or abroad, fearing none but our God,
  We will carve our own pathway to glory.
Then hail the true Red, White, and Blue, —
  The flag of the Constellation!
It sails, as its sailed by our forefathers hailed,
  O'er battles that made us a nation.

Peace.

BY H. E. PRESCOTT.

H that the bells, in all the silent spires,
　　Would clash their clangor on the sleeping air,
Ring their wild music out with throbbing choirs,
　　Ring peace in everywhere!

Oh that this wave of sorrow surging o'er
　　The red, red land, would wash away its stain,
Drown out the angry fires from shore to shore,
　　And give us peace again!

On last year's blossoming graves, with summer calms,
　　Loud in his happy tangle hums the bee;
Nature forgets her hurt and finds her balms, —
　　Alas! and why not we?

Spirit of God, that moved upon the face
　　Of the waters, and bade ancient chaos cease,
Shine, shine again o'er this tumultuous space,
　　Thou that art Prince of Peace!

The Flag.

BY JULIA WARD HOWE.

THERE'S a flag hangs over my threshold, whose
folds are more dear to me
Than the blood that thrills in my bosom its earnest of liberty;
And dear are the stars it harbors in its sunny field of
blue
As the hope of a further heaven, that lights all our dim
lives through.

But now, should my guests be merry, the house is in
holiday guise,
Looking out through its burnished windows like a score
of welcoming eyes.
Come hither, my Brothers who wander, in saintliness and
in sin;
Come hither, ye pilgrims of Nature! my heart doth invite
you in.

My wine is not of the choicest, yet bears it an honest
brand;
And the bread that I bid you lighten, I break with no
sparing hand.

But pause, ere you pass to taste it: one act must accom-
   plished be, —
Salute the flag in its virtue, before ye sit down with me.

The flag of our stately battles, not struggles of wrath
   and greed;
Its stripes were a holy lesson, its spangles a deathless
   creed.
'Twas red with the blood of freemen, and white with the
   fear of the foe;
And the stars that fight in their courses 'gainst tyrants
   its symbols know.

Come hither, thou son of my mother! we were reared in
   the self-same arms;
Thou hast many a pleasant gesture, thy mind hath its
   gifts and charms.
But my heart is as stern to question as my eyes are of
   sorrows full:
Salute the flag in its virtue, or pass on where others rule.

Thou lord of a thousand acres, with heaps of uncounted
   gold,
The steeds of thy stall are haughty, thy lackeys cunning
   and bold.

I envy no jot of thy splendor, I rail at thy follies none:
Salute the flag in its virtue, or leave my poor house
    alone.

Fair lady with silken flouncings, high waving thy stain-
    less plume,
We welcome thee to our banquet, — a flower of costliest
    bloom.
Let an hundred maids live widowed to furnish thy bridal
    bed;
But pause where the flag doth question, and bend thy
    triumphant head.

Take down now your flaunting banner; for a scout comes
    breathless and pale,
With the terror of death upon him: of failure is all his
    tale.
"They have fled while the flag waved o'er them; they've
    turned to the foe their back;
They are scattered, pursued, and slaughtered; the fields
    are all rout and wrack."

Pass hence, then, the friends I gathered, a goodly com-
    pany;
All ye that have manhood in you, go, perish for Liberty.

But I and the Babes God gave me will wait with uplifted
hearts,
With the firm smile ready to kindle, and the will to per-
form our parts.

When the last true heart lies bloodless, when the fierce
and false have won,
I'll press in turn to my bosom each daughter and either
son;
Bid them loose the flag from its bearings, and we'll lie
down to rest
With the glory of home about us, and its freedom locked
in our breast.

"Our Guiding Stars."

BY ORPHEUS C. KERR.

THE planets of our flag are set
　　In God's eternal blue sublime;
Creation's world-wide starry stripe
　　Between the banner'd days of time.

Upon the sky's divining scroll,
　　In burning punctuation borne,
They shape the sentence of the night
　　That prophesies a cloudless morn.

The waters free their mirrors are;
　　And fair with equal light they look
Upon the royal ocean's breast,
　　And on the humble mountain brook.

Though each distinctive as the soul
　　Of some new world not yet begun,
In bright career their courses blend
　　Round Liberty's unchanging sun.

Thus ever shine, ye stars, for all!
   And palsied be the hand that harms
Earth's pleading signal to the skies,
   And Heaven's immortal coat of arms.

The War-Eagle.

BY JOHN NEAL.

THERE'S a fierce gray Bird with a sharpened beak,
 With an angry eye and a startling shriek,
 That nurses her brood where the cliff-flowers blow,
On the precipice top, in perpetual snow,
Where the fountains are mute or in secrecy flow;
That sits where the air is shrill and bleak,
On the splintered point of a shivered peak;
Where the weeds lie close, and the grass sings sharp
To a comfortless tune, like a wintry harp:
Bald-headed and stripped, like a vulture torn
By wind and strife, with her feathers worn
And ruffled and stained; while scattering, bright,
Round her serpent neck, all writhing and bare,
Runs a crimson collar of gleaming hair!
Like the crest of a warrior thinned in the fight,
And shorn and bristling: — see her, where
She sits in the glow of the sunbright air!

With wing half poised, and talons bleeding,
  And kindling eye, as if her prey
  Had suddenly been snatched away,
While she was tearing it, and feeding.

Above the dark torrent, above the bright stream,
The swift ruddy fount, with the changeable gleam,
Where the lustre of heaven eternally plays,
The voice may be heard of the Thunderous Bird
Calling out to her god in a clear wild scream,
As he mounts to his throne and unfolds in his beam;
While her young are laid out in his rich red blaze,
And their winglets are fledged in his hottest rays.

    .   .   .   .   .   .

O ye that afar in the blue air have heard,
As out of the sky, the approach of that Bird!
Have ye seen her, half famished, and up and away,
Her wings in a blaze with the shedding of day, —
Like a vulture on fire! in the track of her prey?

5

"Quaker Loyalty."

BY JOHN G. WHITTIER.

WHY ask for ease where all is pain?
    Shall *we* alone
    Be left to add our gain to gain
When over Armageddon's plain
    The trump is blown?

The levelled gun, the battle-brand,
    We may not take;
But, calmly loyal, we can stand
And suffer with our suffering land
    For conscience' sake.

And we can tread the sick-bed floors
    Where strong men pine,
And down the groaning corridors
Pour freely from our liberal stores
    The oil and wine.

And small shall seem all sacrifice,
    All pain and loss,
When God shall wipe the weeping eyes,
For suffering give the victor's prize,
    The crown for cross!

The Hero of Lake Erie.

BY HENRY THEODORE TUCKERMAN.

N a green knoll in yonder field of graves,
　　Where the rank grass o'er mound and tablet
　　　waves,
A granite shaft allures the vagrant eye
To where the ashes of a hero lie.
This briny air, in its perennial sweep,
Nerved his young frame to conquer on the deep:
Around these shores, a boy, with sportive ease,
He trimmed his shallop to the wayward breeze;
A fearless athlete, in his summer play,
He clove the surf of this unrivalled bay;
Trod the lone cliff where storm-lashed billows roll,
To see the rocks their baffled rage control,
Or watch their serried ranks majestic pour
A ceaseless tribute on his native shore.
The snowy fringes on each leaping surge,
Like victor's wreaths, heroic purpose urge;
In their wild roar the deadly charge he hears,
Feels in their spray a nation's grateful tears;

The mellow sunsets, whose emblazoned crest
With purple radiance flushes all the west,
Like glory's banner, to his vision spread,
To guide the living, consecrate the dead!

His boyhood thus by winds and waves beguiled,
Here Nature cradled her intrepid child;
Won his clear gaze to scan the horizon wall,
His heart with ocean's heart to rise and fall,
His ear to drink the music of the gale,
His pulse to leap with the careering sail,
His brow the landscape's open look to wear,
His eye to freshen in this crystal air:
Braced by her rigors, melted by her smile,
She reared the hero of her peerless isle.

Then went he forth, — not like a knight of old,
Armed at all points, with veterans enrolled;
But in the strength of a devoted will,
A martyr's patience, and a patriot's skill.
No fleet was his whose guns and pennons bore
The tested might of conquests won of yore:
The trees whose shadow played o'er Erie's wave
Were felled and launched, — a rampart for the brave;
The oak that stretched its leafy branches there,
And dallied lightly with the autumn air,

One morn, a sturdy bulwark of the free,
Floated, the empress of that inland sea!
No gray survivors of the battle's wreck
Manned the rude ports of her unpolished deck;
Destined to grapple with a practised foe,
The will to fight is all her champions know.

Sublime the pause, when, down the gleaming tide,
The virgin galleys to the conflict glide:
The very wind, as if in awe or grief,
Scarce wakes a ripple or disturbs a leaf.
The lighted brand; the piles of iron hail;
The boatswain's whistle and the fluttering sail;
The thick-strewn sand beneath their noiseless tread,
To drink the gallant blood as yet unshed;
The long-drawn breath; the glance of mutual cheer,
Eager with hope, oblivious of fear;
Valor's stern mood; affection's pensive sigh, —
Alone declare relentless havoc nigh.
Behold the chieftain's glad, prophetic smile,
As a new banner he unrolls the while;
Hear the gay shout of his elated crew,
When the dear watchword hovers to their view,
And Lawrence, silent in the arms of death,
Bequeathes defiance with his latest breath.*

* Just before the action, a flag with the motto, "Don't give up the ship!" was hoisted.

Why to one point turns every graceful prow?
What scares the eagle from his lonely bough?

A bugle-note far through the welkin rings,
From ship to ship its airy challenge flings,
Then round each hull the murky war-clouds loom,
The lightnings glare, the sullen thunders boom;
Peal follows peal, and, with each lurid flash,
The tall masts shiver, and the bulwarks crash;
The shrouds hang loose, the decks are wet with gore,
And dying shrieks resound along the shore.
As fall the bleeding victims, one by one,
Their messmates rally to the smoking gun;
As the maimed forms are sadly borne away
From the fierce carnage of that murderous fray,
A fitful joy lights up each drooping eye
To see the starry banner floating high,
Or mark their unharmed leader's dauntless air
(His life enfolded in his loved one's prayer) :*
Pity and high resolve his bosom rend,
" Not o'er *my* head shall that bright flag descend!"
With brief monition, from the hulk he springs,
For a fresh deck his rapid transit wings;
Back to the strife exultant shapes his way,
Again to test the fortunes of the day.

* Perry said, after his miraculous escape, that he owed his life to his wife's prayers.

As bears the noble consort slowly down,
Portentous now her teeming cannon frown.
List to the volleys that incessant break
The ancient silence of that border lake!
As lifts the smoke, what tongue can fitly tell
The transports which those manly bosoms swell,
When Britain's ensign down the reeling mast
Sinks, to proclaim the desperate struggle past!
Electric cheers along the shattered fleet,
With rapturous hail her youthful hero greet.
Meek in his triumph, as in danger calm,
With reverent hand he takes the victor's palm;
His wreath of conquest on Faith's altar lays,*
To his brave comrades yields the meed of praise;
With Mercy's balm allays the captive's woe,
And wrings oblation from his vanquished foe!

While Erie's currents lave her winding shore,
Or down the crags a rushing torrent pour,
While floats Columbia's standard to the breeze,
No blight shall wither laurels such as these!

---

* " It has pleased the Almighty to grant to the arms of the United States a
signal victory," &c. — *Perry's Despatch.*

The Flag.

BY GEORGE H. BOKER.

SPIRITS of patriots, hail in heaven again
　　The flag for which ye fought and died,
　Now that its field, washed clear of every stain,
　　Floats out in honest pride!

　Free blood flows through its scarlet veins once more,
　　And brighter shine its silver bars;
　A deeper blue God's ether never wore
　　Amongst the golden stars.

　See how our earthly constellation gleams!
　　And backward, flash for flash, returns
　Its heavenly sisters their immortal beams,
　　With light that fires and burns, —

　That burns because a moving soul is there,
　　A living force, a shaping will,
　Whose law the fate-forecasting powers of air
　　Acknowledge and fulfil!

At length the day, by prophets seen of old,
  Flames on the crimsoned battle-blade;
Henceforth, O flag! no mortal bought and sold
  Shall crouch beneath thy shade.

That shame has vanished in the darkened past,
  With all the chaotic wrongs
That held the struggling centuries shackled fast
  With fear's accursed thongs.

Therefore, O patriot fathers! in your eyes
  I brandish thus our banner pure:
Watch o'er us, bless us, from your peaceful skies,
  And make the issue sure!

The Ship of State.

BY HENRY W. LONGFELLOW.

THOU, too, sail on, O Ship of State!
    Sail on, O Union! strong and great:
    Humanity, with all its fears,
With all the hopes of future years,
Is hanging breathless on thy fate!
We know what master laid thy keel,
What workmen wrought thy ribs of steel,
Who made each mast and sail and rope,
What anvils rang, what hammers beat,
In what a forge and what a heat
Were shaped the anchors of thy hope.
Fear not each sudden sound and shock:
'Tis of the wave, and not the rock;
'Tis but the flapping of the sail,
And not a rent made by the gale.
In spite of rock and tempest's roar,
In spite of false lights on the shore,
Sail on, nor fear to breast the sea:
Our hearts, our hopes, our prayers, our tears,
Our faith triumphant o'er our fears,
Are all with thee, — are all with thee!

National Anthem: God of the Free.

BY WILLIAM ROSS WALLACE.

Air, "*Old Hundred.*"

GOD of the Free! upon thy breath
    Our Flag is still for Right unfurled,
As broad and brave as when its stars
    First lit the darkness of the world.

For Duty still its folds shall stream,
    For Honor still its glories burn;
While Truth, Religion, Valor, guard
    The patriot's sword and martyr's urn.

How glorious is our mission here!
    Heirs of a virgin world are we, —
The chartered lords whose lightnings tame
    The rocky mount and roaring sea.

No tyrant's impious step is ours,
    No lust of power on nations rolled:
Our Flag for *friends* a starry sky;
    For *traitors*, storms in every fold.

Oh, thus we'll keep the Nation's life,
  Nor fear the bolts by despots hurled!
The blood of all the world is here,
  And they who strike us, *strike the world*.

No Slavery shall blast our clime;
  But evermore, on wave and sod,
Only *one* Sovereign's shadow fall, —
  The golden shadow cast by God.

God of the Free! our Nation bless
  In its strong manhood as its birth,
And make its life a Star of Hope
  For all the struggling of the Earth.

Then, shout beside thine Oak, O North!
  O South, wave answer with thy Palm!
All in our Union's heritage
  Together sing the Nation's psalm!

The Flag.

BY LUCY LARCOM.

LET it idly droop, or sway
   To the wind's light will;
 Furl its stars, or float in day;
   Flutter, or be still !
It has held its colors bright
   Through the war-smoke dun;
Spotless emblem of the Right,
   Whence success was won.

Let it droop in graceful rest
   For a passing hour, —
Glory's banner, last and best;
   Freedom's freshest flower!
Each red stripe has blazoned forth
   Gospels writ in blood;
Every star has sung the birth
   Of some deathless good.

Let it droop, but not too long!
   On the eager wind
Bid it wave, to shame the wrong, —
   To inspire mankind
With a larger human love,
   With a truth as true
As the heaven that broods above
   Its deep field of blue.

In the gathering hosts of hope,
   In the march of man,
Open for it place and scope:
   Bid it lead the van,
Till beneath the searching skies
   Martyr-blood be found
Purer than our sacrifice
   Crying from the ground;

Till a flag with some new light
   Out of Freedom's sky
Kindles through the gulfs of nigh
   Glory yet more high.
Let its glow the darkness drown!
   Give our banner sway
Till its joyful stars go down
   In undreamed-of day!

After All.

BY WILLIAM WINTER.

THE apples are ripe in the orchard;
   The work of the reaper is done;
And the golden woodlands redden
   In the blood of the dying sun.

At the cottage-door the grandsire
   Sits, pale, in his easy chair,
While the gentle wind of twilight
   Plays with his silver hair.

A woman is kneeling beside him:
   A fair young head is prest,
In the first wild passion of sorrow,
   Against his aged breast;

While far from over the distance
   The faltering echoes come
Of the flying blast of trumpet
   And the rattling roll of drum.

Then the grandsire speaks, in a whisper,
  "The end no man can see;
But we give him to his country,
  And we give our prayers to Thee." . . .

———

The violets star the meadows,
  The rosebuds fringe the door,
And over the grassy orchard
  The pink-white blossoms pour.

But the grandsire's chair is empty;
  The cottage is dark and still;
There's a nameless grave in the battle-field,
  And a new one under the hill;

And a pallid, tearless woman
  By the cold hearth sits, alone;
And the old clock in the corner
  Ticks on with a steady drone.

The Union, — Right or Wrong.

BY GEORGE P. MORRIS.

IN Freedom's name our blades we draw;
    She arms us for the fight:
For country, government, and law,
    For Liberty and Right.
The Union must — shall be preserved;
    Our flag still o'er us fly:
That cause our hearts and hands has nerved,
    And we will do or die!

Then come, ye hardy volunteers,
    Around our standard throng;
And pledge man's hope of coming years, —
    The Union, — right or wrong!
The Union — right or wrong — inspires
    The burden of our song:
It was the glory of our sires, —
    The Union, — right or wrong!

6

It is the duty of us all
  To check rebellion's sway;
To rally at the nation's call, —
  And we that voice obey.
Then, like a band of brothers, go,
  A hostile league to break;
To rout a spoil-encumbered foe,
  And what is ours retake.

So come, ye hardy volunteers,
  Around our standard throng,
And pledge man's hope of coming years, —·
  The Union, — right or wrong!
The Union — right or wrong — inspires
  The burden of our song:
It was the glory of our sires, —
  The Union, — right or wrong!

The Flag.

BY B. P. SHILLABER.

NOT most, 'mid native airs outthrown,
  Of war or peace, our pride inflames
For that dear flag whose sway we own,
  That our devoted homage claims.

Although its bright and airy folds
  Float from the mast in pictured grace,
Not there alone its glory holds,
  In loving eyes, its highest place.

But where it streams, 'neath foreign skies,
  Our nation's emblematic sign,
To fainting hearts and dimming eyes
  Its stripes and stars are most divine.

The failing pulse exults once more,
  Like to a harp but newly strung,
If to the airs that waft us o'er
  The blazoned gossamer is flung.

'Tis then, forgetting care and pain,
  A momentary joy inures,
And, 'neath its precious folds again
  Is virtue of a thousand cures.

Ah! priceless is its value, where
  The heart in dark desponding gropes;
When failing health installs despair
  Upon the graves of ruined hopes:

'Tis then a wave of wafted love
  From those most precious to our eyes,
A gleam of glory from above,
  A gonfalon of Paradise.

Our Land and its Memories.

BY CHARLES T. BROOKS.

FROM Dan to Beersheba of this our land
Of promise have I passed, from strand to strand;
Have seen the moon o'er Campo Bello rise,
And watched the sun in far South-western skies,
What time his fiery axle, wheeling slow,
Stood on the reddening Gulf of Mexico.
Slowly I've labored, with the panting steam,
Up Mississippi's tortuous, turbid stream,
Where, at each bend, each wood-crowned sweep, behold
Sea after sea its noble bays unfold!
There, in the glimmering dusk, when far-off trees
Like spectres stand, the cheated vision sees
Strange shows of fleets and fleet-girt cities, rife
With all the stir of busy human life.
Mark, as by magic, Orient Stamboul rise!
Its bristling masts, a forest, meet your eyes,
Where, half of sight and half of fancy born,
Wind the bright waters of the Golden Horn.

And now, 'mid hoary, reverend groves we glide,
Where Gunga's thousand islets break the tide;
Where, robed with pendant moss, the aged trees
Stand like the priests of Nature's mysteries.
Fades each fair vision with a puff of steam,
As onward still we labor up the stream.
But, lo! where, in her stateliness and pride,
Looks out o'er all the valley, far and wide,
That young queen city, " thronèd by the West,"
What visions of the future fire the breast!
Eastward she looks; and seems, with noble eye,
Her proud Atlantic sisters to defy,
And glow in the great race and rivalry.
With reverent step and swelling heart I've pressed
The boundless prairie of the teeming West;
And where the northern lakes, a mighty chain,
Stretch their bright links along our vast domain,
There have I travelled, — there, transported, seen
Blue inland oceans, piny oceans green.
And where New England's Alps majestic rise,
I've climbed that rocky island in the skies,
Whence, seen afar, our noble rivers glance
Like threads of silver in the broad expanse;
And where earth seems a living map — no more —
Dotted with towns, with forests speckled o'er.
And I have stood, and felt a nameless thrill

Of reverence and rapture, on the hill,
Where, calmly looking down on the fair shore
Of Chesapeake and stately Baltimore,
In emblematic, marble majesty,
Stands Washington, "in the clear, upper sky,"
And breathes his benediction.

                     Have not we
A goodly heritage from sea to sea,
From lake to gulf?   What noble rivers pour
Their inland tribute to the extended shore!
O'er rolling upland and on waving plain,
By town and farm, what peace and plenty reign!
And must the day come when fraternal war
Shall rend our mighty empire, star from star?
Or (worse) Corruption's canker eat the chain
No earthly arm had power to snap in twain?
Must the day come, when over freemen's graves
Their shameless sons shall walk, the slaves of slaves?
When the proud flag, whose field of starry blue
Tells of the sky, whence our young Freedom drew
Her life's first breath, — the flag, whose stripes of red
Tell of the brave who at her summons bled, —
Shall droop inglorious, or dishonored lie,
A taunt, a jest, a sign of infamy?
Benignant Heaven, forbid ! and ye, whose dust
Our soil, " from Maine to Georgia," holds in trust !

Forbid it, living sons of those dead sires,
Who lit on Freedom's heights the morn-watch-fires,
Whose heart's blood, when they fell, enriched the sod,
And scattered seed of valor far abroad,
That, mouldering in full many a furrow, lies,
Our nobler harvest, ripening for the skies!
Gone is the day when our young eagle heard
The cry of war, and in his eyrie stirred;
When Quincy saw the blood-red dawning nigh,
And Warren, at the call, made haste to die;
When Otis, Adams, fanned the kindling flame,
And Hancock pledged a patriot merchant's name;
Gone is the day, — compatriots, never more
May dawn its like! — when, ghastly-red with gore,
Yon altar-height the smoke of sacrifice
Sent up, in summer sunlight, to the skies.
Gone is the day; and, oh, not soon may men
Beat back the ploughshare to a sword again!
Yet warfare, brothers, is our honored lot,
A warfare that, while life lasts, endeth not.

.

America.

BY CHARLES K. TUCKERMAN.

IN pride of youth and high behests,
   She stands magnificently fair;
For honor heaves her mountain breasts,
   And freedom lifts her forest hair:
Like one she looks, who, fresh from strife,
   Feels on his brow the wreath of fame
Press fresh ambition into life,
   Fresh need to wear a deathless name.

In face a child; in mien a queen;
   Unlineaged, yet of high degree, —
One feels a crown would but demean,
   And rank a less condition be.
Hers is the diadem of respect,
   The sceptre of the innate will;
Her task a nation to erect,
   A destiny sublime fulfil.

As roams the restless eagle's eye
　　That cleaves an azure realm new found,
Uncertain whether next to fly,
　　Discerning not a final bound,
She gazes on her fair estate,
　　Then shakes the hands of either sea,
And, through the elemental great,
　　Forefeels the greatness yet to be.

Exultingly she waves her stars,
　　And stands transfigured to her feet:
No more red War her glory mars,
　　And dims a vision else complete.
Transfigured to her feet she stands, —
　　Those feet where late the strangled veins
Ran blackened blood, and iron bands
　　Mocked at the cursèd clank of chains!

Oh, sad sweet feet! oh, pitiless chains,
　　Sad relic of a former fate!
Freedom's foul fetters — slavery's gains —
　　Dwarfing the else transcendent great.
Long did ye wear them; ah, too long!
　　Proud limbs bowed down with sin and shame,
Weak where thy nature made thee strong,
　　Nameless where most deserved a name.

" And who shall cast them off, and when?"
    Long, long did wisdom seek in vain;
And weary heart and voice and pen
    Asked it, and asked it yet again.
But they shall ask it never more:
    His answer shook the land and sea;
Peace rode upon the wings of War,
    And God hath set the Nation free.

Aye free, great land, from South to North,
    From lake to gulf, from coast to coast!
Thy vaunted liberty henceforth
    Shall be no more an empty boast:
Yet guard it with a faithful hand, —
    Let not the Spirit mock the Form;
Watch well the winds that sweep the land,
    From baffling breeze to sudden storm.

Advance thy stately standard high,
    Till, in each white and ruddy line,
The far-off nations can descry
    A holy hope, a saving sign.
Advance it till the mingling rays
    Of new-born stars crowd out the night,
Making the azure field one blaze
    Of inextinguishable light.

Wounded unto Death.

BY CHARLES A. BARRY.

 FEW steps more; just down by the bushes;
  And then, — the prayer that's 'haunting my
   lips, —
Will they mind it up yonder, when my soul pushes
 Out o' this suddenly awful eclipse?
There goes the surgeon: no need to hail him, —
 I'm safe for a dead 'un at next roll-call.
This is a job that would certainly fail him:
 Give me a drink, Jack, — Lord help us all!

Never a saint, and it's no use whining:
 I've got to travel, — I'll do my best;
The game's played out, and there's no divining
 What'll become o' me and the rest.
I'm wishing the parson was here to cheer me,
 For it's little o' Christian speech I know.
It's coming! — if only SHE was near me,
 (God bless her!) I'd be willing to go.

All the long night, lad, I lay a dreaming, —
   A dream that stuck like a stab in my brain.
I told the boys under the bayonets gleaming,
   This morning, I'd never be with 'em again:
They called me a muff, and swore I was shamming, —
   Quick came the tears, spite of all I could do, —
Lord! when they saw me led out, there was damning:
   I'll bet you they missed me, an' pitied me too.

Drop me down in this bed o' sweet clover.
   Thanks: cut the rigging off o' my breast.
Bide a bit, comrade: 'twill shortly be over, —
   To-morrow I'll camp in the land o' the blest.
Yon goes a shell! — that's jolly good humming!
   Over the hill the old gal breaks:
Lift me a little, — death surely is coming!
   Give us your fist, — see how my hand shakes!

'Twas only a faint! — not much in a hurry
   Above there, I take it, for fellows like me.
Listen, old chap: you'll see that they bury
   This body o' mine right decently;
And comfort the old folks, — worse than the darting
   Pain o' this bullet's the thought o' that blow.
God help 'em! and keep 'em through the long parting!
   I shall see 'em on t'other side, you know!

And here's the traps I intrust to your keeping:
 Her letters ˙ (the portrait must go, Jack, with me)!
Ah, lad, there'll be plenty o' wailing and weeping
 In the old homestead down by the sea!
But tell 'em I died with th' harness all on me,
 In th' face o' th' foe, in the heat o' the blast,
With never a stain of dishonor upon me: .
 You'll tell 'em, dear Jack, I was true to the last.

For we two have toted like brothers together,
 Hard-tack and water, this many a day.
Did ever I show the least bit o' white feather?
 Bully for you! — I thought 'twould be nay.
Battle and march and civic procession!
 Steady, boys! — give 'em a touch o' the steel!
Here, at the end of a soger's profession,
 'Tis the Red, White, and Blue, come woe or come weal.

It's getting dark, and I'm off for certain!
 Kiss me, dear Jack, for I cannot see:
I'm called *this* time, and they'll drop the curtain,
 As sure as shooting, betwixt you and me.
Ah, well! they'll give me a place, I reckon,
 Among the boys that have gone before!
Good-by, good-by, old fellow! they beckon —
 The angels — on the opposite shore!

FRUITS OF FREEDOM

The Old Blue Coat.

BY BISHOP BURGESS OF MAINE.

YOU asked me, little one, why I bowed,
    Though never I passed the man before?
  Because my heart was full and proud
  When I saw the old blue coat he wore:
    The blue great-coat, the sky-blue coat,
    The old blue coat the soldier wore.

I know not, I, what weapon he chose,
  What chief he followed, what badge he bore;
Enough that, in the front of foes,
  His country's blue great-coat he wore:
    The blue great-coat, the sky-blue coat,
    The old blue coat the soldier wore.

Perhaps he was born in a forest-hut;
  Perhaps he had danced on a palace-floor;
To want or wealth my eyes were shut,
  I only marked the coat he wore:
    The blue great-coat, the sky-blue coat,
    The old blue coat the soldier wore.

It mattered not much if he drew his line
　From Shem or Ham in the days of yore;
For surely he was a brother of mine,
　Who for my sake the war-coat wore:
　　The blue great-coat, the sky-blue coat,
　　The old blue coat the soldier wore.

He might have no skill to read or write,
　Or he might be rich in learnèd lore;
But I knew he could make his mark in fight:
　And nobler gown no scholar wore
　　Than the blue great-coat, the sky-blue coat,
　　The old blue coat the soldier wore.

It may be he could plunder and prowl,
　And perhaps, in his mood, he scoffed and swore;
But I would not guess a spot so foul
　On the honored coat he bravely wore:
　　The blue great-coat, the sky-blue coat,
　　The old blue coat the soldier wore.

He had worn it long, and borne it far;
　And perhaps, on the red Virginian shore,
From midnight chill till the morning star,
　That warm great-coat the sentry wore:
　　The blue great-coat, the sky-blue coat,
　　The old blue coat the soldier wore.

When hardy Butler reined his steed
   Through the streets of proud, proud Baltimore,
Perhaps behind him, at his need,
    Marched he who yonder blue coat wore:
      The blue great-coat, the sky-blue coat,
      The old blue coat the soldier wore.

Perhaps it was seen in Burnside's ranks,
   When Rappahannock ran dark with gore;
Perhaps on the mountain-side with Banks,
    In the burning sun, no more he wore
      The blue great-coat, the sky-blue coat,
      The old blue coat the soldier wore.

Perhaps in the swamps 'twas a bed for his form,
   From the seven days' battling and marching sore;
Or with Kearney and Pope, 'mid the steely storm,
    As the night closed in, that coat he wore:
      The blue great-coat, the sky-blue coat,
      The old blue coat the soldier wore.

Or when right over him Jackson dashed,
   That collar or cape some bullet tore;
Or when far ahead Antietam flashed,
    He flung to the ground the coat that he wore:
      The blue great-coat, the sky-blue coat,
      The old blue coat the soldier wore.

7

Or stood at Gettysburg, where the graves
   Rang deep to Howard's cannon roar;
Or saw with Grant the unchained waves,
   Where conquering hosts the blue coat wore:
      The blue great-coat, the sky-blue coat,
      The old blue coat the soldier wore.

That garb of honor tells enough,
   Though I its story guess no more;
The heart it covers is made of such stuff,
   That the coat is mail which that soldier wore:
      The blue great-coat, the sky-blue coat,
      The old blue coat the soldier wore.

He may hang it up when the peace shall come,
   And the moths may find it behind the door;
But his children will point, when they hear a drum,
   To the proud old coat their father wore:
      The blue great-coat, the sky-blue coat,
      The old blue coat the soldier wore.

And so, my child, will you and I,
   For whose fair home their blood they pour,
Still bow the head, as one goes by
   Who wears the coat that soldier wore:
      That blue great-coat, the sky-blue coat,
      The old blue coat the soldier wore.

The Empty Sleeve.

BY DAVID BARKER.

Inscribed to General Howard, of Maine, who lost his right arm in defence of his country.

B Y the moon's pale light, to a gazing throng
Let me tell one tale, let me sing one song:
'Tis a tale devoid of an aim or plan;
'Tis a simple song of a one-arm man.
Till this very hour, I could ne'er believe
What a tell-tale thing is an empty sleeve;
What a wierd, queer thing is an empty sleeve.

It tells, in a silent tone, to all
Of a country's need and a country's call;
Of a kiss and a tear for a child and wife,
And a hurried march for a nation's life.
Till this very hour, who could e'er believe
What a tell-tale thing is an empty sleeve;
What a wierd, queer thing is an empty sleeve?

It tells of a battle-field of gore,
Of the sabre's clash, of the cannon's roar;
Of the deadly charge, of the bugle's note,
Of a gurgling sound in a foeman's throat;
Of the whizzing grape, of the fiery shell,
Of a scene which mimics the scenes of hell.
 Till this very hour, would you e'er believe
 What a tell-tale thing is an empty sleeve;
 What a wierd, queer thing is an empty sleeve?

Though it points to a myriad wounds and scars,
Yet it tells that a flag with the stripes and stars
In God's own chosen time will take
Each place of the rag with the rattlesnake:
And it points to a time when that flag shall wave
O'er a land where there breathes no cowering slave.
 To the top of the skies let us all then heave
 One proud huzza for the empty sleeve;
 For the one-arm man, and the empty sleeve.

NOTE. — The foregoing was written one moonlight evening while General Howard was addressing a large throng from the steps of the Bangor House, and his empty sleeve was every now and then floating on the breeze. — D. B.

Our Flag.

BY ORPHEUS C. KERR.

FLAG of my country! Standard of the free
　　In every land where dwelleth Liberty!
　　Thou fairest page the eye of Light can find,
Turned by the quivering fingers of the wind;
Charter of Hope by God to mortals given,
Bright with the planetary pomp of heaven;
Still to the patriot a recorded prayer,
Lingering in sweet suspense upon the air, —
Let me within thy broad protection stand,
And read thine honors for my native land.

As from the shattered temple of the storm
Springs the grand arch of light in fairest form,
Splits the black dome 'mid distant thunder's din,
And, through the shadows, lets the sunshine in;
So thou, my country's banner, didst arise
From a dead storm whose battles shook the skies, —
Rose, like the coming day's memorial shield,
From a red sunset's torn and bleeding field,

Dipped in the starry mine, whose clusters bright,
Drawn to a Union, beamed the perfect light.

Born of the battle, nursling of the wind,
Symbol of strength unfurled for all mankind,
Through the dark hour that brings our brothers' shame,
Still from our altars rise, a beacon flame,
Pride of the air!   Thou solitary spar
Cast to the sea, whose waves the whirlwinds are,
Scarce the faint wretch thy signal stars descries
When a new life is kindled in his eyes:
Nerved with a might dividing fates to dare,
Boldly he cleaves the billows of despair,
Clasps thee in triumph to his heaving breast,
And drifts securely to a haven rest.

Proudest of flags that mount the giddy mast,
Coy to the breeze, defiant to the blast,
Blazoned aloft in every zone and clime,
Sheath for the sword, or badge for harvest time;
Spread at command of cannon's deadly throat;
Fluttering in play to merman's liquid note, —
Whether thy hues in polar vapors freeze,
Or blend with sunset on the Southern seas,
Still thy broad folds shake deathless honors down
On the free head too proud to wear a crown;

Still to God's image, be he bond or free,
Thou art a birthright of Equality!

And shall this sacred leaf in Glory's tome,
Plucked from the volume storying Nature's dome,
And a great Nation's grand appeal to God
For the blest power to break a tyrant's rod,
Be by the hands of its own bearers riven, —
Torn and despoiled the heraldry of heaven?
At the fell thought, what darkness falls around!
See the red streams flow gurgling from the ground!
Blood of our fathers, hallowing every spot,
Are the grand lives poured out in thee forgot?
Shades of the mighty! can thy dead eyes see
Brother to brother curse thy legacy?

Hark! from the North what sullen murmurs come!
And from the South wells up a mournful hum;
Soft through the East the muffled drums resound,
And in the West a dead command goes round.
Hark to the tramp of ghostly armies four,
Through the long grass bedewed with heroes' gore!
From the red hill where Warren's soldiers bled,
From the dark fens where slumber Marion's dead,
From the free plains where Scott's battalions fell,
From the dread field whose tale let Britons tell, —

Onward they come, in all the dead array
Of a slain army on the Judgment-day.

Well for the land whose maddened sons would dare
Trample in dust the signet of the air;
Well for the land whose impious purpose known
Robs of its weight the grim funereal stone, —
That as the hosts, from beds of ages called,
Turn their pale faces to the skies appalled,
Full from the nation's Capitolic dome
Beam the Republic's stars amid the gloom:
Still they all shine, and still the stripes defend, —
These for the foe, those for the trusty friend.

As the dead army mark the starry shrine,
Sounds of thanksgiving thrill along the line; .
Swiftly the arms to set position come,
And the salute is answered by the drum;
Then, as the templed shadows fall away,
Waves the old Flag in all the glow of day.
Gone are the hosts, no more to trouble men,
Till the last trumpet sounds the march again.

Flag of the Fallen! Standard of the Dead!
Thee let me follow with unwavering tread:
Free from the touch of slave and tyrant fly;

And, when thou fadest, let a nation die!
Bond of the Freeman! sacred with the blood
Shed by brave men for brave men's noblest good,
Say to the eye that looks to God and thee
From a scorned trust, or fell captivity, —
Stripes for the traitor, foe, and honor's ban;
Heaven for the patriot and the honest man!

Union and Liberty.

BY OLIVER WENDELL HOLMES.

FLAG of the heroes who left us their glory,
　　Borne through their battle-fields' thunder and
　　　flame,
Blazoned in song, and illumined in story,
　　Wave o'er us all who inherit their fame!
　　　　Up with our banner bright,
　　　　Sprinkled with starry light;
Spread its fair emblems from mountain to shore:
　　　　While, through the sounding sky,
　　　　Loud rings the Nation's cry, —
Union and Liberty! one evermore!

Light of our firmament, guide of our Nation,
　　Pride of her children, and honored afar,
Let the wide beams of thy full constellation
　　Scatter each cloud that would darken a star!
　　　　Up with our banner bright, &c.

Empire unsceptred! what foe shall assail thee,
  Bearing the standard of Liberty's van?
Think not the God of thy fathers shall fail thee,
  Striving with men for the birthright of man.
      Up with our banner bright, &c.

Yet if, by madness and treachery blighted,
  Dawns the dark hour when the sword thou must draw,
Then, with the arms to thy millions united,
  Smite the bold traitors to Freedom and Law!
      Up with our banner bright, &c.

Lord of the Universe! shield us and guide us,
  Trusting thee always through shadow and sun:
Thou hast united us, — who shall divide us?
  Keep us, oh keep us, the *Many in One!*
      Up with our banner bright,
      Sprinkled with starry light;
Spread its fair emblems from mountain to shore:
      While, through the sounding sky,
      Loud rings the Nation's cry, —
Union and Liberty! one evermore!

Our Country.

BY HARRIET M°EWEN KIMBALL.

DEAR Land! we crown thee with our praise,
    In patriot pride we name thee;
With loyal lips we sing thy lays;
    With swelling hearts we claim thee.
Yet lofty speech and stirring song
    Alike are unavailing,
While hands of treachery and wrong
    Thy glory are assailing.

But loyal steel defends thy fame,
    And writes, in crimson letters,
A pledge that turns to endless shame
    The threat that Treason utters.
And, from the loyal cannon's mouth,
    The lightning-flash and thunder
Repeat to traitors, North and South,
    "*The bond ye cannot sunder!*"

We mourn thy blood-stains, Father-land!
   But War's wild clash is better
Than Peace, that yields a craven hand
   To Treason's iron fetter;
Till from New England's crystal hills
   To Georgia's bloom of cotton,
Proud Victory's breath our banner fills,
   The white flag be forgotten!

The Old Flag Over-sea.

BY HENRY MORFORD.

KNOW not how the absence fell
 Of that my eyes so sought with longing, —
The dear old flag we loved so well
 When traitor hands were wronging;

For still, thank God! it droops and waves
 Where'er the winds of commerce woo it,
Or deed of despot, scourging slaves,
 Demands that we undo it.

But weeks, for me, since Consul's staff
 Had shown the striped and starry streamer,
Or it had blown from frigate's gaff,
 Or peak of sailing steamer.

The meteor flag of Britain here;
 And there an ensign broader, fuller,
And bruiting victories quite as dear, —
 The Emperor's tricolor.

It seemed to me, though dim and far,
　　And scarce embodied forth in thinking,
My own dear land, with stripe and star,
　　To nothingness was sinking;

That I should know my home no more,
　　However sought, through toils and dangers,
But, weary, tread some foreign shore,
　　And live and die 'mid strangers.

And then one morn I wound my way
　　Down Calton Hill of Edinboro',
With Holyrood my goal to-day,
　　And Stirling Carse to-morrow;

With Arthur's Seat that skyward laughed,
　　And the grim Castle piled defiant;
Till one full cup of eld I quaffed,
　　That made my dull veins riant.

" Who would not stay from native land,"
　　I said, " for this, so famed in story? —
These memories of the Iron Hand,
　　And gleams of kingly glory?"

Who would not?   Pause! — for, up a spire,
  Against the blue void sheer and utter,
Azure and white and ruddy fire,
  I saw a banner flutter.

It was my own, — *our* own!   O Heaven!
  How the quick throb that love convulses,
When some dear recognition's given,
  Went bounding through my pulses!

How all my native land at once
  Sprang back to being in the shimmer,
With those whose absence had for months
  Made every daylight dimmer!

The gray old driver on his box
  Saw the quick glance, the tear-drop starting:
A smile, whose kin the heart unlocks,
  His sun-browned lips was parting.

"Hech, mon!" he said, "I ken the sight
  That maks the saft'nin' mood come o'er ye!
'Tis a bonnie flag! — I've seen the light
  In other eyes before ye.

" Ye'r far frae hame, and weel may spare
    Ane drap to wat yer country's honor;
For sad's the load — ay, sad and sair —
    Rebellion laid upon her.

" Ay, I could a'most greet mysel'
    To see a thing so braw and bonnie,
And think what faes hae wished it ill,
    Yet floatin' high as ony!"

I reached and grasped the driver's hand,
    I choked with grateful, mournful feeling:
The home-flag in a foreign land
    Had brought a new revealing, —

How round a simple bunting-strip,
    In cost a song, in weight a feather,
A mere *mouchoir* for lady's lip,
    A nation's pride can gather.

A father's fondness for his child,
    A lover's tender, pleading passion,
A patriot's flame, — all form one wild
    Unreasoning adoration.

8

" God bless the dear old bannered fold !
   God keep the hosts who own and guard it!
Till plucked its hues, when time is old,
   By the same Hand that starred it! "

So shouted I down Calton Hill,
   And the old Gael's pleased murmur follows;
And such the shout I'll echo still
   Upon the soil it hallows.

To float it, Western winds blow free;
   And blue bend Western skies above it:
But it needs the Old Flag Over-sea
   To know how much we love it!

AIRDCHFANOCROCHAN, HIGHLANDS OF SCOTLAND,
     August 8, 1865.

Pæan for Victory.

BY EDWARD P. NOWELL.

SHOUT, shout the tidings o'er
  The land, from shore to shore, —
    All shall be free!
The Knights of Bondage bleed;
Rebellion's ranks recede;
Our arms triumphant lead
    To victory!

All hail the glorious sight!
Columbia's martial might
    Traitors astounds!
Fair Freedom's valiant host
Has silenced Slavery's boast
Along Secessia's coast,
    And through her bounds!

God grant we soon may see
Enduring unity,
    And sheathe the sword:
Our country's foemen felled,
Secession's spirit quelled,
The smoke of strife dispelled,
    And Peace restored!

Then Union's banner bright
Shall herald Freedom's light
    On shore and sea;
And Heaven's benignant rays
Illume the Nation's days, —
Our hearts ascribing praise,
    Great God! to thee.

The Flag.

BY J. ROLLIN M. SQUIRE.

 O FLAG, still proudly dost thou wave
Above the free, above the brave!
And on thy folds, that kiss the air,
Behold! morn's opal streaks are there,
Blent with the hues that warm the skies
When pallid day from evening flies,
Ere the red sun removes his crest
That floods with fire the burnished West.

The night comes on, yet thou dost share
The unclouded beauty radiant there;
For on thy blue is star on star,
Thrice burnished in the flame of War,
As bright as those that glitter where
The night her mantle trails in air;
And of thy shining throng not one
Has lost its light, — not one is gone.

Oh, proudly float in every breeze
That sweeps the land or curls the seas!
The world, how haughty, fierce, or cold,
Thy heavenly hues in every fold
Will recognize, and bow to thee,
Untarnished emblem of the free,
Red with the blood thy patriots gave
To strike the shackles from the slave.

No longer shall thy ruddy bars
Be likened to the bleeding scars
The bondmen wore, before the sea
Of strife rose up and set them free:
But in thy spaces, white and red,
The world shall recognize, instead,
And chant the song, of glorious note,
In strife conceived, in Victory wrote.

After the War.

BY MRS. ANN S. STEPHENS.

OH, say not that war-times were brighter than
        these,
        When banners are torn from the warriors that
        bore them!
Oh, say not the ocean, the storm, and the breeze
    Are proudest and grandest when war thunders o'er
        them!
For the battle's hot light grows pale to the sight
When the pen wields its power, or thought feels its might.
Now mind rules triumphant where slaughter was red,
And the glory of peace crowns our Bald Eagle's head.

May the blessings of concord in harmony rise;
    Let the sword keep its sheath and the cannon its
        thunder;
Let brotherhood reign from the earth to the skies,
    And love link the States that war could not sunder.

Where mermaids still weep and pearls lie asleep,
The flag of disunion no longer shall sweep;
Our flag waves triumphant from ocean to shore,
And its stars light the nests of our eagles once more.

As a Niobe, folding deep grief to her breast,
    The nation has mourned o'er the children's dissension:
She called upon Heaven, like a mother distressed,
    And the great God of Battle gave his intervention.
We feel with a start the quick pulse of her heart,
And she is no more from her children apart.
For peace reigns triumphant, our people are one,
And our Bald Eagle soars with his eyes to the sun.

The blood that is kindred throbs kindly once more:
    The glow of our joy fills the earth and the ocean;
It leaps on the waves, and it sings on the shore,
    Till the globe, to its poles, feels the holy commotion.
Let us join in our might to be earnest for light;
Where the Saxon blood burns, let it ever be right:
For our eaglets are nested in glory and love,
While peace reigns triumphant, and God reigns above.

The Great Bell Roland.*

BY THEODORE TILTON.

Suggested by President Lincoln's First Call for Volunteers.

TOLL! Roland, toll!
   In old St. Bavon's tower,
   At midnight hour,
The great bell Roland spoke,
And all who slept in Ghent awoke.
What meant the thunder-stroke?
Why trembled wife and maid?
Why caught each man his blade?
Why echoed every street
With tramp of thronging feet,
   All flying to the city's wall?
   It was the warning call
That Freedom stood in peril of a foe!
And even timid hearts grew bold
Whenever Roland tolled,
And every hand a sword could hold,

---

* The famous bell Roland, of Ghent, was an object of great affection to the people, because it rang to arouse them when liberty was in danger.

And every arm could bend a bow!
    So acted men
    Like patriots then, —
Three hundred years ago!

    Toll! Roland, toll!
Bell never yet was hung,
Between whose lips there swung
So grand a tongue!
    If men be patriots still,
    At thy first sound
    True hearts will bound,
    Great souls will thrill!
Then toll, and strike the test
Through each man's breast,
And let him stand confest!

    Toll! Roland, toll!
Not now in old St. Bavon's tower,
Not now at midnight hour,
Not now from River Scheldt to Zuyder Zee,
    But here, — this side the sea, —
    Toll here, in broad, bright day!
      For not by night awaits
      A foe without the gates,
    But perjured friends within betray,

Who do the deed at noon!
Toll! Roland, toll!
Thy sound is not too soon!
To arms! Ring out the Leader's call!
Re-echo it from East to West,
Till every hero's breast
Shall swell beneath a plume and crest!
Toll! Roland, toll!
Till cottager, from cottage-wall,
Snatch pouch and powder-horn and gun!
The sire bequeathed them to the son,
When only half their work was done!
Toll! Roland, toll!
Till swords from scabbards leap!
Toll! Roland, toll!
What tears can widows weep
Less bitter than when brave men fall?
Toll! Roland, toll!
In shadowed hut and hall
Shall lie the soldier's pall,
And hearts shall break while graves are filled.
Amen! so God hath willed!
And may his grace anoint us all!

Toll! Roland, toll!
The Dragon on thy tower
Stands sentry to this hour,

And Freedom yet is safe in Ghent!
  And merrier bells now ring,
And, in the land's serene content,
  Men shout, "God save the King!"
Until the skies are rent!
    So let it be!
    A Kingly King is he
    Who keeps his people free!
    Toll! Roland, toll!
Ring out across the sea!
No longer They but We
Have now such need of thee!
    Toll! Roland, toll!
Nor ever let thy throat
Keep dumb its warning note
Till Freedom's perils be outbraved!
    Toll! Roland, toll!
Till Freedom's flag, wherever waved,
Shall shadow not a man enslaved!
    Toll! Roland, toll!
From Northern lake to Southern strand!
    Toll! Roland, toll!
Till friend and foe, at thy command,
Shall clasp again each other's hand,
And shout, one-voiced, "God save the land!"
And love the land that God hath saved!
    Toll! Roland, toll!

Spirit of the Union Soldiers.

BY MILES O'REILLY.

BE merciful to the South!
　　Not with the empty word in your mouth;
　　But merciful be — let your actions tell —
To the men who were beaten, but fought so well:
　　Be merciful to the South!

　　Be merciful, — and be more, —
Now that the red days of battle are o'er;
For, when the first cause of the quarrel is sought,
No clean hands by us into court are brought:
　　Be merciful to the South!

　　Be merciful to the South!
Gentle in deed and in word of mouth;
For no craven brand on the forehead shines
Of the men who met us in volleying lines,
　　And fought for the flag of the South.

We are all here at last,
The terrible days of our struggle past;
And again the old banner floats elate
O'er the capitol dome of each Sister State,
          In the North, East, West, and South!

          Be merciful to the South!
For slaughter and ruin and hunger and drouth
They have suffered who made such a gallant fight
For a cause that was wrong, but they thought it was
     right:
          Be merciful to the South!

Peace.

BY PHŒBE CARY.

LAND, of every land the best!
    O land, whose glory shall increase!
Now in your whitest raiment dressed
    For the great festival of peace, —

Take from your flag its fold of gloom,
    And let it float undimmed above,
Till over all your vales shall bloom
    The sacred colors that we love.

On mountain high, and hill-top low,
    Set Freedom's beacon-fires to burn,
Until the midnight sky shall show
    A redder pathway than the morn.

Welcome, with shouts of joy and pride,
    Your veterans from the war-path's track:
You gave your boys, untrained, untried;
    You bring them men and heroes back!

And shed no tear, though think you must
   With sorrow of your martyred band, —
Not even for him whose hallowed dust
   Has made our prairies holy land.

Though, by the places where they fell,
   The places that are sacred ground,
Death, like a sullen sentinel,
   Paces his everlasting round;

Yet, when they set their country free,
   And gave her traitors fitting doom,
They left their last great enemy
   Baffled beside an empty tomb.

Not there, but risen, redeemed, they go,
   Where all the paths are sweet with flowers:
.They fought to give us peace; and, lo!
   They gained a better peace than ours.

JULY 4, 1865.

WHAT GOD HATH JOINED TOGETHER

E PLURIBUS UNUM.

UNITED STATES

LET NO MAN PUT ASUNDER

Union.

BY ALBERT LAIGHTON.

DARK and sullen o'er the Nation lowers
 Fell Disunion, like a tempest cloud:
  Shall its lightnings rend this land of ours?
  Shall it be the Country's sable shroud?

Shall a band of traitors rashly sunder
 Ties so firmly woven by the free?
No! the echo rolls, in tones of thunder,
 From the mountain passes to the sea.

By the many hopes the living cherish,
 By our faith in Freedom's sacred trust,
By the sainted names that cannot perish,
 By the soil made dear by patriot dust,

By the noble deeds enshrined in story,
 By the voices speaking from the Past,
By our priceless heritage of glory, —
 We'll defend the Union to the last!

Abraham Lincoln.

BY MRS. JULIA WARD HOWE.

CROWN his blood-stained pillow
  With a victor's palm;
Life's receding billow
  Leaves eternal calm.

At the feet Almighty
  Lay this gift sincere
Of a purpose weighty,
  And a record clear.

With deliverance freighted
  Was this passive hand;
And this heart, high-fated,
  Would with love command.

Let him rest serenely
  In a Nation's care,
Where her waters queenly
  Make the West most fair.

In the greenest meadow
　That the prairies show,
Let his marble's shadow
　Give all men to know, —

" Our first hero, living,
　Made his country free;
Heed the second's giving, —
　Death for Liberty."

Cambridge : Stereotyped and Printed by John Wilson & Son